attitude devant

third position

arabesque

sous-sus

jeté

fourth position

temps levé

second position

AMERICAN BALLET THEATRE
presents

My Daddy Can Fly!

by **Thomas Forster** with **Shari Siadat**

illustrated by **Jami Gigot**

RANDOM HOUSE STUDIO ▲ NEW YORK

The dress-up corner is Ben's favorite part of his classroom. This morning, his friends Rachel, Louise, Daniel, and Jayden are busy talking about what they are going to be when they grow up.

Rachel wraps a black silk ribbon around her waist and says, "Hi-YA! I'm going to be a tae kwon do master."

In a hard hat and fluorescent vest, Jayden says, "I'm going to be an architect and design a cozy hamster house for Snuggles."

Picking up a pile of books, Daniel says,
"I'm going to be a teacher like Mr. Underwood."

"I'm going to be a doctor," Louise says, putting a stethoscope around her neck, "just like my auntie."

"Well, when I grow up, I'm going to fly,
just like my daddy," says Ben.

"Wait? Your daddy can fly?" asks Daniel.

"Oh, oh, he's a pilot!" Jayden says. "My mommy is a pilot, too."

"Nope, my daddy isn't a pilot . . .

"...but he can fly."

"And he's super strong," says Ben.

"Is he a football player?" guesses Louise.

"A firefighter?" Rachel wonders out loud.

"I know! He's a furniture mover!" shouts Jayden.

"Can he lift a piano?"

"Nope," says Ben. "He's not a football player or a firefighter. And he is not a furniture mover, and I'm pretty sure he couldn't lift a piano . . .

"... but he's stronger than anyone I know.

"My daddy is as fast as a hummingbird . . .

"... but slower than a sloth.

"Daddy can be fierce like a tiger . . .

". . . but he can also be gentle
like a butterfly."

Ben looks at his friends. "Any more guesses?"

Louise, Rachel, Daniel, and Jayden stopped guessing. They were thinking.

Ben gives them a few more clues.

He jumps.

He turns.

He points his toes and leaps.

Ben lifts the heaviest book he can find over
his head and spins. He does a pirouette, and his
friends gasp at how quickly Ben moves his feet.

Finally, Ben bends to one knee, lifts his arms oh so gently above his head, and then lowers them to his sides.

"A ballet dancer! Your daddy is a ballet dancer!"
Rachel, Louise, Jayden, and Daniel scream out.

Mr. Underwood and every student in the class have
stopped what they were doing and are watching Ben.
   "And so is Ben!" Mr. Underwood exclaims. "Bravo, Ben!"
   "Bravo!" the whole class says together.

A Note from Thomas Forster

Growing up in southeast London, I would never have guessed that one day I would become a principal dancer with American Ballet Theatre. When I was eight years old, I loved the Teenage Mutant Ninja Turtles and really wanted to take karate. According to my mum, I was too young to join the local karate class, so she enrolled me in ballet classes instead. I never did end up taking karate, and ballet turned into my passion. I was fortunate to attend the Elmhurst Ballet School and later graduated from the Royal Ballet's Upper School with honors. I was then offered a job in New York City to dance for American Ballet Theatre. I have performed all over the world and in front of thousands of people. I have been lucky to have the support of teachers, friends, and family to help me achieve my dream. I encourage any boys or girls with a passion for dance to work hard and chase your dreams, too. Like my grandad would always tell me, "If at first you don't succeed, try and try again."

Cheryl Arron in Hackney London

When I was seven years old, I auditioned for the Royal Ballet School's Junior Associates Program.

Johann Persson

Here I am at age eighteen, when I graduated from the Royal Ballet School and got my dream job with ABT Studio Company.

Rosalie O'Connor

I remember watching my idols dance this ballet, On the Dnieper, *when I first joined ABT. This photo is from when I had the opportunity to perform it myself at the Metropolitan Opera House.*

Rachel Forster

My sister Louise and I are pictured here on Selsey Beach. She has Down syndrome and is a dancer with a company called Magpie Dance, a dance charity in the UK for people with learning disabilities. Louise is by far my favorite dancer in the world.

Sara Letschert

November 12, 2016, is the day my son, Benjamin Thomas Forster, was born.

Sara Letschert

Here, Benjamin's mum, Leann Underwood, and I are taking Ben on a stroll on the waterfront in downtown Jersey City.

Leann Underwood

This is my son, Benjamin Thomas Forster. Ben, whatever your personal goal is in life, do your best and never stop trying. The sky's the limit.

first position

plié

tendu

sauté

attitude derrière

effacé devant

fifth position

pirouette